WHISPERS
ON THE
Waves

11 Feb. 2021

To Ezra,
I trust that you will enjoy the short
stories that these local critters have to
tell. Please thank your granpa Tom
for supporting me. All the best,
Kim

KIM MANN

Whispers on the Waves
Copyright © 2019 by Kim Mann

Tellwell Talent
www.tellwell.ca

ISBN
978-0-2288-1742-0 (Hardcover)
978-0-2288-1741-3 (Paperback)
978-0-2288-1743-7 (eBook)

Prologue

Sincere gratitude goes to The Alan Parsons Project and their instrumental song *Dream Within a Dream*, introductory lyrics narrated by Orson Welles. Edgar Allen Poe wrote the original poem.

"For my own part, I have never had a thought which I could not set down in words with even more distinctness than that with which I conceived it.

There is, however, a class of fancies of exquisite delicacy which are not thoughts, and to which as yet I have found it absolutely impossible to adapt to language.

These fancies arise in the soul, alas how rarely. Only at epochs of most intense tranquility, when the bodily and mental health are in perfection, and at those weird points of time, where the confines of the waking world blend with the world of dreams.

And so I captured this fancy, where all that we see, or seem, is but a dream within a dream."

Whispers on the Waves

Kim Mann

The short stories in the following collection entitled *Whispers on the Waves* are a work of fiction. Names, characters, places, and incidents are the products of the writer's imagination, and any resemblance to actual animals, living or dead, events, or locales is entirely coincidental. The details of ecological processes and principles are based on best known peer-reviewed facts substantiated by the writer's personal experiences.

The writer has taken the liberty to partially anthropomorphize his cerebral critter companions, but only to the extent that they can express human-like feelings and emotions, and communicate with a "universal" language. In all other respects, they present themselves in their natural states, as the wild animals that they are. And, of special note, where appropriate they present their challenges of sharing their natural habitats with us human animals.

Table of Contents

Protagonists

Roberta "Bobby" Bear

Bobby

Born: 24 June
Age: 20 (approximately 50 human years, 2.5:1)

Nurturer, teacher, protector. Very loyal, empathetic, and sociable. Guided by her emotion and heart. Is intuitive and compassionate.
Bobby has a strong sense of family, culture, lineage, and heritage.

Ollie Otter

Ollie

Born: 30 May
Age: 4 (approximately 26 human years, 6.5:1)

A gentle, affectionate, and curious individual. He is very sociable, chats with nearly anyone and is always ready for fun. However, in contrast, Ollie has a tendency to suddenly get serious, thoughtful, and restless. It is age-appropriate that Ollie can be impetuous, irreverent, and a bit reckless. He is fascinated with his world, is often inspiring, exciting, passionate, and never boring.

Reginald Regal Eagle I "Reggie"

Reggie

Born: 25 August
Age: 26 (approximately 65 human years, 2.5:1)

A loyal, steadfast, practical, and very wise old soul with a need to serve others. He has a meticulous attention to detail. Reggie has a deep sense of life, spirituality, unity, and the interconnectedness of everything. At times rather pompous, he has a powerful and imposing character. Reggie can become overly concerned about matters that nobody else seems to care much about.

Ms. Katie Cougar

Katie

Born: 06 January
Age: 7, (approximately 35 human years, 5:1)

Is very serious by nature, responsible, traditional, fiercely private, and independent. Ms. Katie is a master of self-control and is highly skilled; her accomplishments are a direct result of her experience and expertise. She is very intelligent with philosophical and intellectual tendencies.

Of Whales, Barnacles, and Steep Pebble Beaches

It was a beautiful and breezy summer afternoon in a sheltered and secluded bay along the west coast of their island. Ollie and Bobby were doing what they most frequently love to do, just lolling about. From Bobby's comfortable resting spot at the base of a huge hemlock tree on this south-facing slope that overlooked the bay, she gazed down upon her sleeping friend, Ollie. He was the very model of restful repose. Such a fine specimen, as river otters go, in the prime of his life, living life to the fullest whether working, playing, eating, chattering, or relaxing. At times Ollie could be raucous and impetuous, and on occasion a bit reckless, but to Bobby he was simply her youthful, playful, ever lovable companion and confidante, her friend. As fine a young river otter as ever there was.

Although river otters and black bears, on first impression, would seem unlikely companions because they both enjoy solitary lifestyles, Bobby couldn't help thinking how much she and Ollie enjoyed each other's company. She found this all the more interesting when she considered how different they were in so many ways. Bobby has long been conscious that she embodies the spirit of her black bear ancestors, and their great strength and courage. Her mother had been a steadfast grounding force in Bobby's early life. She had also been a great healer and teacher. And Bobby had obviously inherited her mother's great size. Why, Bobby couldn't even remember ever being called by her given name, Roberta. As a cub she had grown so rapidly in stature and strength that she frequently overpowered her brother and cousins in play, and had equally rapidly earned the name Bobby.

This secluded bay was one of their favorite places because it had so much to offer. The warm summer sun bathed the secluded and protected bay. Snow-covered mountain peaks highlighted the background. The bay was calm compared to the entrance that connected it to a large strait. The waters in the bay's entrance were quite choppy. Bobby imagined what the conditions would be like on the beautiful exposed beaches further up the coast. She visualized huge rolling waves, having come all the way from the other side of the Great Ocean, roaring ashore and pounding down on the steep pebble beaches. She was in awe of such tremendous force and raw power. Such memories were imprinted on her mind, as they were in the minds of her ancestors.

While savoring her thoughts and memories, Bobby rose from her restful spot to stretch. She needed to check about, to sniff the air as it drifted down from behind them. Finding nothing to smell, nothing to see or hear, her feelings of comfort and security were restored. The direct sun had warmed her black summer coat about to the limit of her comfort, so she needed to move into the shade for a while. But first, she needed a good old fashioned back scratch. As she looked about for a suitably coarse tree trunk, she paused to observe her travelling companion, Ollie.

There he lies, stretched out on his back, on a small mossy ledge on the slope just below her. His cheeky upside down face staring at nothing. His pale, softly furred belly exposed to the warmth of the sun. This is a remarkably quiet moment for her chatterbox friend, she thought. Ollie is a picture of peace and tranquility.

Bobby ambles over to a giant Douglas fir, in anticipation of a delightfully sensuous scratch. As she rises on her hind legs and leans back against the coarse bark of the great tree, she takes in the entire vista of the bay, from the calm waters of the rocky lee shore just a few steps below Ollie, over a few small islands, to the forested shorelines surrounding the rest of the bay. And now to business. She slowly squats on her haunches and rises again to her full height, feeling the ridges of the bark press deeply into her back. She repeats these moves, up and down, in ecstasy.

Feeling fully satisfied, Bobby strolls over to a soft, shaded, needle-covered spot. Movement below suddenly catches her attention. It's Ollie. The heat of the day must be getting to him, too. He goes through his familiar stretching routine, arching his neck and back while extending his hind legs, one at a time, as far back as he can. Having fully extended his long slender body and graceful muscles, Ollie looks up at Bobby, a reassuring look that says all is well in their world. Ollie steps then slides on his belly down over the moss, steps and slides again, down to the rock slope. His last step and slide sees him plop beneath the surface of the water for a much-needed cooling dip. As Bobby watches the trail of little bubbles that follow Ollie's underwater passage parallel to the shoreline, she ponders his amazing ability to swim so swiftly and stay underwater for so long. How very different their perspectives of their worlds are, and yet how similar. Bobby finds herself missing the sounds of him, his companionship, his chatter.

As quickly as Ollie plops into the water, he suddenly reappears and scampers back to his favorite mossy mat. As he dries himself on the moss and begins grooming his magnificent fur with his clawed webbed paws, he says, "And how are you doing on this amazingly fine afternoon, Bobby?"

"Fine, thank you, and so kind of you to ask," replies Bobby. "It is so sheltered and serene in this bay. Have you noted how choppy it is at the entrance, and beyond out into the strait?"

"Yes Bobby, I would not be so comfortable on any of the exposed shorelines this afternoon. Perhaps later this evening or tomorrow morning we could wander out again," ventures Ollie.

"That's very interesting Ollie; while you were resting I had been thinking of a particularly exposed beach, often mentioned by my elders. This beach, which is much farther up our coast, features prominently in our collective memory. A great aunt or uncle once told of an amazing event that occurred on this rather remote and unique beach. Although this ancestor has long since passed on, the story of this event has been passed down among my kind for generations."

"What's so unique about this beach?" inquired Ollie. "What is this fascinating process?"

"As you wish Ollie," replied Bobby. "As you know, beaches have many different characteristics, ranging from very shallow with fine smooth sands, to very steeply sloping beaches with coarse pebbles, depending on their orientation and exposure to the powerful prevailing westerly winds driving the open ocean waves. You and I prefer the more sheltered, sandy or silty beaches where our foraging efforts are more richly rewarded and where you most frequently find your delicious mud worms. This beach in my story is unique because of its combination of steepness, coarseness, and remoteness. It is particularly important, as it turns out, to our whales."

"Oh do please carry on my dear Bobby, you have my undivided attention and ever-increasing curiosity," said Ollie. "Remote, steep pebble beaches and whales, what else?"

"Well yes, Ollie, there is yet another critter entwined in this amazing account: our acorn barnacle, the same ones so common to us along our rocky shores at low tides. These are the barnacles that are solidly cemented to the rocks and are uncomfortably sharp to walk on. This story answers one of our questions but leaves us with yet another mystery. Let me explain," Bobby implored.

"As you and I have observed many times while watching whales feeding, sleeping, or simply travelling near shore, some of them are heavily encrusted with barnacles. Why, we have even commented that these barnacles must be uncomfortable and impede their smooth passage through the water. Well Ollie, one of my ancestors was foraging well above the high tideline of this beach, for the steepness and coarseness of the rounded pebbles makes it very difficult to walk along, and there's usually little to be found there any way that she would not have seen from above. As she climbed a small rise, she looked down to see an adult female gray whale washed up on the beach. Her first thought was that the whale was sick, injured, or dying. A large wave hit her quite forcefully and pushed her well up onto the beach. The whale offered no resistance. Her great mass just slowly slid down over the coarse pebbles and back into the water. The whale floated away, only to be shoved ashore again by the powerful waves. The whale appeared to have given up to a brutal fate, being repeatedly driven up onto the beach."

"How sad," commented Ollie. "But the end must come to us all eventually, and not all endings are peaceful."

"Ah yes, so true Ollie," replied Bobby, "But, amazingly, this was not the case here. This was not an ending. This was a fascinating and ongoing process, as we have come to understand it. This whale was not sick or injured, but just living her life as it was apparently meant to be."

"So," said Ollie "what is this fascinating ongoing process?"

"Just as it seemed that an ending was about to occur," continued Bobby, "the whale showed a sudden surge of life. As she began to swim away from the shore, it became obvious what the whale was doing. The side of her that had scraped along the beach was—amazingly— scoured of all the barnacles. She was clean and smooth again. She swam about for a short while, then came back to the beach and presented her other, heavily encrusted side. The contrast was astounding. And the process began again, continuing to completion over the next several minutes until she was fully free of barnacles. My ancestors decided that this interaction between whales, barnacles, and steep pebble beaches has likely been going on for eons, and will likely continue to do so," concluded Bobby.

"I agree, Bobby," said Ollie, "and thank you for sharing that insightful knowledge. But at the outset you mentioned there is yet another mystery. How is that so?" inquired Ollie.

"Well, you see Ollie, it has never been explained to me, nor have I ever been able to figure out, how barnacles, so solidly cemented to the rocks, manage to get from the rocks onto the hides of the whales. And furthermore, why would they want to do so?" replied Bobby.

"Yes Bobby, that is an imposing mystery," conceded Ollie. "Perhaps I could share some thoughts and observations, and together we might be able to come up with some plausible explanations."

"Firstly, let me share some of my personal experiences with the huge grays. Some of these encounters have not been very pleasant or positive for me. When these grays return to our waters in the summer to feed, they are ravenously hungry. They have travelled a very long way. I understand they, as well as humpbacks, spend their winters along the southern shores of our continent way to the south of us. How they make such long journeys without rest or food is another mystery, but every summer they reappear.

"Many of these grays share the same waters where I like to forage and feel about with my dextrous and tactile clawed fingers. The soft seabed in these shallow places are very productive and provide great feasts of mud worms and other juicy morsels. The waters in my favourite foraging places are usually much warmer than the deeper areas, and yet not too deep for me to dive down to. This is where I have come into conflict with the grays a couple of times.

"You see Bobby, these huge critters swim along the bottom of the seabed on their sides, and use the sides of their long snouts to root out these same tasty treats. In so doing, they stir up such great clouds of silt and sediments that I can't see a thing. I have to give up and go in search of another place to find food."

"That's fascinating Ollie," said Bobby. "And yet I can understand how frustrating and futile such a conflict must be. I had no idea what a wonderful and challenging world you disappear into when you flip your long thick tail skyward and dive beneath the surface. You are an amazing critter my dear Ollie. How fortunate I am to have you share these perspectives with me," declared Bobby.

"Well Bobby, we all live and learn; it sure beats the alternative," Ollie remarked. "And I've learned from this, too. I've learned to avoid this conflict. The presence of these grays is obvious from a distance. When they surface for air, which all mammals must eventually, they have a distinctive blow. The twin blow holes in the tops of their heads produce their characteristic V or heart shaped pattern of spray if it's not too windy. On seeing this sign, I don't even bother foraging in these waters for a while, they're just too murky, and the little critters remaining in the seabed are just too disturbed."

I understand and accept everything that you have shared with me about these gray whales Ollie, but I can't imagine what their feeding behavior in your waters has to do with the mystery of the migrating barnacles," queried Bobby.

"Well Bobby, I'll get to that directly, I just wanted to establish the presence of these Gray whales in our warm shallow waters, with tons of tasty treats to eat, at this time of the year," replied Ollie. "I have observed other very interesting goings-on in these waters during the early summer that may also have some relevance."

"Okay Ollie, you've piqued my interest now too, so please keep going," insisted Bobby.

"Well," began Ollie, with a dreamy, faraway look in his eyes, "a few seasons ago, when a much younger river otter lived in my skin, it was a bright sunny day such as this. While slowly rising to the surface from a delightful dive, savoring the moment, and marveling at the sun's rays penetrating the water all the way to the bottom, I looked up and around and made an astounding observation. The rays of the sun were highlighting gazillions of very tiny little critters, like shrimp tinier than I ever would have imagined possible. I saw many other tiny wiggly things, as tiny as the finest grains of sand on a beach. I had never noticed anything like it before. It was like discovering a whole new world within a world. I was so taken by my discovery that I almost forgot about the little crab I was bringing ashore for lunch. Ever since that fortunate event, I have made a point to watch for the gazillions of tiny wiggly things."

"That's fascinating Ollie," declared Bobby. "Such vivid images, which I can totally relate to."

"How can that be Bobby?" questioned Ollie. "I've never even seen you swim. You can't dive."

"No no, of course not, silly," replied Bobby, with a coarse rumbling chuckle. "Please allow me to explain. You see, my dear Ollie, many seasons ago, when a much younger black bear lived in my fur coat, I had a similar experience. We were deep in the forest. I had been watching my brother scratching about a large boulder. He had found a few tasty grubs and other delectable little treats. Our mother had been watching him too, and she decided to lend a hand. Actually, much more than a hand. Our mother was a very large bear—even larger than I am today. She leaned her great weight into that bolder, and with apparent ease, rolled it over. We discovered gazillions of tiny, crawly, wiggly, little critters—it was a whole new world within my world! It is a wonderful world that we live in, Ollie. But, I didn't mean to get us off course Ollie, I'm sorry. Please continue," said Bobby. "I'm excited to learn what these gazillions of tiny wiggly things might have to do with our barnacles and whales."

"Okay," Ollie continued, "over my few seasons of life, I have come to understand that, mainly during the spring, tiny eggs can be seen almost everywhere, especially attached to blades of eelgrass, or in a jelly-like substance attached to rocks or larger kelp plants. A cousin once shared that, while diving for crabs, he had checked out a small den near the base of a rock wall. He saw the tiniest little octopuses he had ever seen emerging from the entrance to the den. On peering deep inside the den, he was amazed to discover a big octopus tending thousands and thousands of eggs hanging in clusters from the top of the den. She looked very pale and sickly. My cousin didn't stick around, he needed to surface for air. But his story has added to my belief these teeny octopuses must also be a part of the great masses of miniature living things that I had been seeing in the water column. Also at these times of the year, the waters become all clouded up, all white and milky. In due course, the gazillions of these tiny, free-swimming things can be seen. I'm pretty sure that this mass of miniature life is where the filter feeders, like the anemones, the sea jellies, and even the great filter-feeding whales must get their food."

"But, the most amazing thing, Bobby, is that some of these free-swimming specks actually come from the most unlikely critters, such as mussels, tube worms, and even our many barnacles. Come to think of it, on shallow dives searching for crabs, I have even seen barnacles giving off small milky white clouds. These white clouds could have contained the earliest free-swimming forms of baby barnacles. So presumably, Bobby, a few of these tiny tots that don't get eaten by other filter feeders must eventually grow up, settle onto a suitable surface, and develop into their more familiar adult forms."

"Ah!" declared Bobby. "Different forms. I think I get it. Like the eggs in a pond that hatch into pollywogs or tadpoles then grow up to be frogs or toads. Or, like the eggs on branches of bushes that hatch to be caterpillars, then grow up to be butterflies or moths. Fascinating, Ollie. I understand. We may be onto something here, Ollie. But why would barnacles ever want to attach themselves to a whale?"

"Very good question, Bobby," said Ollie. "Right off the top of my tiny mind, I can think of at least two answers. These answers, when you think of it, are common to all of us. They are related to protection and food."

"We are making great progress with our mystery Ollie," said Bobby excitedly. "Have you noticed, time seems to have stopped? Where has the afternoon gone? Do keep going."

"Well," continued Ollie, "Even hanging around with you offers me some protection. I just remembered that incident late last summer when I came under a sudden threat. I had just surfaced with a large Dungeness crab and was carrying it up from the beach to a sheltered spot beneath an overhang of trees, when, apparently from nowhere, two of the coastal wolves came trotting along in the shallow water next to the shore. It became immediately apparent that they intended to get between me and the safety of the water. It seemed that I was done for. Then, just in the nick of time you appeared from the nearby berry bushes. Whew! Was I ever glad to see you. Those menacing marauders had an immediate change of heart. You saved my life. I had never thought of our relationship in that way before; nor will I ever forget it, Bobby. And likewise, I believe that the whales offer the barnacles some protection, too."

"How so?" queried Bobby. "I thought barnacles were pretty much indestructible and inedible."

"Oh no, Bobby," responded Ollie, "barnacles have predators too. Sea snails, mussels, and sea stars enjoy a feed of fresh barnacle. These critters may not move very fast, but there are many of them, and they have very large appetites. In spite of the barnacles' crusty coats of armor, they can still be penetrated and eaten. But a barnacle living on a whale would have much more protection."

"And just think on that for a moment, Bobby. Barnacles are filter feeders, too, so being firmly fixed to a giant filter feeder such as a whale without teeth, provides a free ride to unlimited supplies of food. They enjoy the best of all worlds."

"Yes," agreed Bobby, "at least until the whale feels that it's time to get cleaned up again, and heads off to visit one of the steep pebble beaches."

"So true!" chuckled Ollie. "Endings come to each and every one of us, eventually."

"I do declare," said Bobby, "that we have found reasonable and probable answers to our little mystery of whales, barnacles, and steep pebble beaches."

"And I do declare," said Ollie, "since we also seem to have frittered away the whole afternoon, it is high time that we went in search of some supper." They rose, stretched, and ambled off along a familiar old trail.

Ms. Katie Goes to Sea

It was a gorgeous, bright, clear summer morning on the west coast of the big island. The wind was calm, and the sea was only gently disturbed by the constant Great Ocean swells. And there it was again, plain for all to see, an ancient relic of an old wooden lifeboat or skiff probably lost at sea long ago. Amazingly, it was still relatively intact and had fetched up on this isolated, shallow, muddy, silty bar. Fully exposed by the low tide, the bar was blanketed by a lush covering of vibrant pale green lettuce kelp.

Ms. Katie Cougar had suddenly encountered four black-tailed deer foraging out on the kelp and immediately set upon them. She was rewarded with one of the smaller ones, and her breakfast was served up. As she was finishing her meal, she noticed that the anticipated entourage of second-comers had arrived. A couple of young wolves were hanging back by the salal bushes beneath the trees, and several herring gulls had begun circling overhead. A few of them had landed and were hopping closer and closer, as if to say, "Hurry up now, it's our turn next." Being sufficiently sufficed, with a full tummy, Ms. Katie moved on along the bar, relinquishing her leftovers, for such is the way of it in the natural order of things. All must strive to survive.

And besides, while eating, Ms. Katie watched this intriguing vessel. This old wooden skiff had probably been washed up on this silty bar a long time ago on a huge king tide associated with the proximity of the big moon. The relic life raft was now very high and dry.

In a single, smooth, agile movement, Ms. Katie leapt onto the gunnel and peered down into the open boat. Other than some bilge water, the vessel was empty. But, a long, wide, thick plank thwart amid ship looked most inviting. It well might have seated three or more persons at some past moment in time. But at this moment, the skookum seat had already absorbed a significant amount of heat from the brilliant morning sun and felt delightful when she delicately touched it with her paw.

Before she knew it, she was stretched out, full length, under the clear blue windless sky, soaking up the sun's boundless energy. The raucous cackling and screeching cacophony of the ravenous herring gulls faded as Ms. Katie drifted away, figuratively and literally, as the flood tide swiftly approached another all-time annual high water mark.

The rapidly increasing flood of yet another king tide covered the bar in its timeless rhythmic cycle. The rising water imperceptibly refloated the old skiff. The endless Great Ocean swells that had fetched all the way from the other side of the ocean were very low and gentle on this calm sunny morning and caused the boat to rock ever so gently, taking Ms. Katie deeper and further away into her restful slumber— and deeper and farther away from shore, too.

As the big island began heating up with the approach of midday, the air above it rose, thereby setting up the typical afternoon on- shore breeze, and adding to the gentle ocean swells. In turn, this added to the rocking of the little, soft chined vessel. The increased rocking and rolling, combined with the sloshing of the bilge water in the bottom of the hull were the first sensations that Ms. Katie became aware of as she began her return from wherever she had been in her deep restful slumber. *Where am I?* she wondered as she raised her head and peered over the gunnels.

"Oh, my!" she said in instant shock. She was wide awake.

The shore seemed impossibly far away. And it wasn't even the same stretch of shore where she had so recently eaten breakfast. Little did she know, the kelp covered bar was now underwater, as would any other intertidal features be, especially during king tides. Nothing looked familiar.

Oh, my! Oh, my! What to do? What to do? She immediately recognized the need to control her emotions. Fear and panic can be life-threatening. *Must be calm and rational,* she thought.

As Ms. Katie pondered her predicament she became aware of the vastness of the Great Ocean. It seemed to be timeless, at least there was no sense of time that she could perceive. And it seemed that there were no references out there, at least none that were familiar to her. It was so different from the myriad of ever-changing sights, sounds, and smells of the shores and forests beyond. She was at sea. She was in awe. It was a totally new experience for Ms. Katie. And she was quite disoriented.

As the summer sun intensified she became aware of an acute feeling of aloneness. Not loneliness exactly, after all, she lived a solitary life, and yet, she had never felt this alone before. There had always been a busyness about her, whether it be other critters or insects, the breeze moving the branches about her, passing smells on the air, or the ever-changing sounds. She had always felt at one with her surroundings, never feeling as alone and apart from it as she did now. This was not a comfortable feeling. She had to get control of it.

Breathe, embrace, believe, Katie, she said to herself as she inhaled deeply. *Reach out and connect with your new environment. Everything will be fine. Believe.*

As she embraced this new approach to her situation, she took stock of the ever-changing sky and clouds, the slapping of the waves against the hull, the saltiness of the sea air, and the continuous movement of the old skiff. She embraced it all. The more she looked, the more she saw. A couple of common terns raced by. One of them stopped, hovered, and plunged headfirst into the water. A lone black-footed albatross, with a massive wingspan, gracefully skimmed over the surface of the sea, never seeming to flap those great wings at all. Even the shoreline in the distance was changing, or realistically, she in her skiff was moving relative to the shoreline. Another interesting perspective.

In spite of her best efforts to breathe, embrace, and believe, Ms. Katie still felt a niggling sense of despair. She accepted the omnipotence of nature and how little, if any, control she had over whether she would live through this ordeal or die horribly at sea. These weighed heavily.

In a final and desperate effort to restore stability and hope, she refocused her attention toward shore. She observed, almost imperceptibly, that she seemed to be getting closer to a long stretch of bluffs. Way above the bluffs, riding high on the rising warm air currents, only slightly larger than a speck, was a familiar soaring sight. "Yes. It is. A majestic bald eagle," she said.

Could it be? Could it possibly be? she wondered as she followed its flight.

Yes, yes, it very possibly could be, she realized as the eagle turned away from the bluffs and began a gradual descent out to sea directly toward her. As the eagle's flight path seemed more certain, Ms. Katie recognized her old friend, Reginald Regal Eagle I, or Reggie as she called him.

From high above the bluffs, soaring on the thermals, Reggie conceded; he just had to check it out. *Were his old eagle eyes finally starting to deceive him?* he thought. As he continued his gradual descent from altitude toward this strange apparition, his faith in his eyesight was restored. Yes, it was an old wooden skiff adrift over a mile offshore. And there was what appeared to be a familiar form sitting on the thwart.

Could it be? Could it possibly be? he wondered. It sure looks like it. *Yes! Yes! It is her! My old friend Ms. Katie.* Reggie made a low pass over the little vessel and saw Ms. Katie's huge bright eyes smiling up at him in welcome. Reggie circled back toward shore, downwind. When his height above the water seemed just about right, he completed his circle toward Ms. Katie again, and into the on-shore breeze. He was now perfectly set up on final approach for a graceful two-point landing onto the prow of the old skiff.

With a brief flurry and folding of his wings, Reggie and Katie faced each other and shared a tender visual embrace.

"Fancy meeting you like this, Katie," said Reggie. "You must have a tale to tell; I cannot imagine. Please do tell."

"I have gotten myself into a most unusual and precarious predicament, haven't I? And yes Reggie, it is a fascinating tale to be sure," declared Katie.

Ms. Katie recounted the details as she understood them, including the associated feelings she had experienced.

"Reggie, I'm wondering if I would simply drift back to shore, leap out of the old skiff and, with pride and dignity restored, just walk back into my old life?" Katie said. "Or would I continue to drift farther and farther away from shore, out of sight of land, eventually to die at sea of thirst and starvation, perhaps losing my mind in the process?

"I realized how little control I had of my fate. How frail and vulnerable I really am. Yes, Reggie, I was just coming face-to-face with my mortality. Flashbacks momentarily brought back my entire life. It was a surreal experience. Thank goodness and mercy for you, Reggie. At least now I am comforted that regardless how this situation works out you, my dear friend, will be with me to the end," said Ms. Katie, as she sighed with relief.

Ms. Katie's tale profoundly affected her dear friend. And she sincerely appreciated the intensity and concentration he brought to bear on his active listening skills.

Reggie continued his prolonged period of silence. He first contemplated Katie and then everything around and above her.

"You have demonstrated a profound acceptance of life in the natural world. Few ever attain such wisdom," stated Reggie. "Let me summarize the meat of the matter, as I understand it."

Reggie made a deep croaking sound as he cleared his throat. "Life, encompassing living, dying, and death, in health and illness, in strength and fragility, is what it is. In this basic precept, we cannot jump higher than our shadow. Acceptance of life, with grace, humility, and dignity is the only truly sustainable alternative.

"Observe the natural world, with silence and stillness in your heart and mind, and the naked truth of this assertion will come to you. What will also come to you is the veracity of the assertion that there are no villains or victims in the natural world. Life is all about survival. This means the survival of those most suited to the perpetuation of their species, and the survival of the very threads of the fabric of the natural world. We are all one.

"This is as it should be. There are no mistakes in the perfect world. Life is a great journey," declared Reggie. "Also, Katie, you were quite correct in stating that I will be with you throughout this. Regardless, however the threads of this event will be woven into the grand fabric of life, I will see you through it to the end.

"And now, Katie, I have a gift I will give to you. This is the gift of an amazing aerial observation platform. I may be gone for a while, but I will return. In the meanwhile, continue to breathe, embrace, and believe."

With that, Reggie turned into the gentle breeze, leaned forward, and with a mighty flap of his great wings, he was airborne and away. First, he headed back toward shore where he quickly flew into the rising heated air over the big island and the powerful thermal currents. Katie watched as he rose higher and higher and finally disappeared into the ever-whitening sky. The sea all around her had become completely calm again except for the very gentle Great Ocean swells. For the next while, without the awareness of the passage of time, Katie sat perfectly still on her big plank seat and contemplated Reggie's words. He surely was a wise and true friend.

Being quite accustomed to extended periods of stillness, Katie continued embracing all about her. As she scanned the skies she noticed they were becoming more gray than white. Then she noticed a tiny black spec way off in the distance, way out to sea. Sure enough, the spec was descending toward her. A growing warmth comforted her. Reggie turned downwind, then turned on final approach, making another perfect two-point landing. He gracefully and majestically perched on the prow.

Reggie stared long and intently at her, then said, "Katie, I have surveyed high, far, and wide. I have only daunting information. Our predicament, at least for the immediate future, is unfortunate. We are about a mile and a half offshore now. We will continue to drift with the ebbing tide and, given our sea level perspective, will soon lose sight of the coast. Sadly, my information just gets more daunting. Our course will soon intersect a tide line whereupon we will pick up an offshore current that will take us a bit farther away from shore, but even farther down the coast."

Katie sat in silent resignation. Nothing further needed to be said. Silence and serenity prevailed.

With the onset of dusk, Reggie suddenly turned on his perch into the slightest breeze, and with a great flap was gone again. Katie watched him gradually turn, in what direction she could not tell, as it had been a while since she had been able to see the coast. He had not attempted to gain much altitude and soon was out of sight. Interestingly, she felt no sense of aloneness because she just knew she wouldn't be alone for long.

After a while, Ms. Katie began to wonder if Reggie had decided to go back to a more familiar and secure roost along the coast for the night, when suddenly—out of nowhere—he reappeared. From a low altitude, he was coming straight at the now very familiar old wooden skiff. With a bit of alarm and concern, she realized that he was rapidly approaching with no intention of landing. He swooped low over the boat and dropped something, which landed with a splash in the bilge water right in front of her. It was a herring about as long as her plank seat was wide.

"Reggie, you are wonderful!" she said. As she tucked into the fish, Reggie circled and sat proudly perched upon his prow, staring intently at her again.

Ms. Katie found great joy and satisfaction in her incredibly delightful dinner and soon ended up licking her paws. In her comfortable state of acceptance, she settled down for the night. Her first night at sea.

"I can't see more than a mile or so," said Katie as she embraced the morning. "At least it's still very calm."

"Agreed," replied Reggie, also fully awake and feeling a bit restless. "But this is sufficient visibility for me to make a reconnaissance flight to reassess our circumstances."

He turned slightly and was gone. He was out of sight almost immediately. Ms. Katie shuddered a bit, shaking off the morning dampness. She stood up on her bench and proceeded with her morning stretching routine, followed by the ritual grooming with her long raspy tongue. As the air around her gradually warmed, the mist dissipated. The visibility increased noticeably. Before long Reggie was back. Proudly perched upon his prow, he began preening and rearranging a few of his flight feathers. When done, he turned and stared intently at Katie once more. She watched, waited, and listened just as intently.

"I have an interesting mix of information to share with you this morning, my dear Katie. We have drifted even farther than I thought we would. A weather system seems to have stalled directly over us, and I am concerned that when it starts to move off toward the big island it will be followed by very strong winds. However, while surveying our surroundings, I happened upon a very interesting situation. There is another boat out here. There are three men aboard and they have sports fishing gear.

I believe that we will soon intersect another tide line. The men aboard that other boat appear to be fishing just outside and along that tide line. I'm not too sure just what to make of it all right now, but it does present some interesting possibilities. We'll just have to wait and see. What will be, will be."

Ms. Katie was in complete acceptance now and warmly comfortable with her lot in life. She was especially interested in Reggie's final words. They were strangely familiar to her. She had heard them somewhere before, but partly in another language, perhaps in another life. She recalled the phrase "Kay Sera Sera," and bits of ancient lyrics, "When I was just a little girl, my mother said to me...." Katie had long ago accepted that there would likely be many things that she would never be able to understand. And that was okay with her. We are who we are. What will be will be.

As the morning wore on, the skies became darker and the breeze freshened. *Reggie is restless again and almost a bit excited, too,* thought Ms. Katie. And then he was gone again. Katie, resigning, curled up on her big plank seat, little knowing that Reggie would not return to her this day.

As Reggie gained altitude he immediately spotted the other boat. It was about a mile or so from the old wooden skiff, and the distance between the boats was gradually closing. The three men were busy about their aft deck and seemed oblivious to Katie's decrepit old skiff. Reggie had to get their attention and distract them from their busyness. *How better to do it?* thought Reggie, as he swooped down and made a surprise, low, high speed pass over their boat.

"Wow! Did you see that?" cried one man. "Never seen the like of it even back home along the coast of Georgia."

"Yeah, but I sure didn't see him comin'," replied another. "What d'y'all suppose that was all about?" said another.

"I reckon he attempted a snatch-and-grab at Bobby Jo's stinky old fishing hat," said the first man.

That comment elicited uproarious laughter as the first fellow continued, "That wouldn't have been as much Bobby Jo's loss as ours, on accounta 'cause we'd a had to look at his ugly, shiny bald head for the rest of this fishin' trip."

Meanwhile, Reggie orbited nearby, just out of their sight, observing the scene below. He gave the three men sufficient time to recover their composure while he set up his next, more explicit communications effort. He lost sufficient altitude to permit him to descend and intersect a direct line, a course between Ms. Katie's skiff and their fishing boat. Once on this course, he applied sufficient flap to the trailing edges of his huge wings to slow his speed, and, raising his head slightly, maintained an altitude of about one hundred feet above the water. Reggie successfully completed a non-threatening over-flight of the sports fishing vessel. He once again had their undivided attention. Reggie turned, reversing course, maintaining altitude and, maintaining the course to Ms. Katie's skiff. He made a second slow flight over the three amazed men, continuing in the direction of the derelict skiff until he was sure that he was out of their sight once again. Reggie gained altitude and sufficient distance to remain out of sight. He soared back and forth while he watched and waited to see if his communications effort had been deciphered.

Aboard the fishing vessel, the men agreed that the big bald eagle apparently had no fear of them, and presented them with no threat, but were all puzzled as to what his bizarre behavior meant.

"Wha'd'ya all s'pose he was tryin' to tell us?" posited one.

"He seems ta be tryin' ta direct our attention ta somthin' over the nor'east," said another.

The fellow who the others referred to as Bobby Jo, pulled his hat down tightly over his bald head and offered, "S'pose he's tryin' to direct us to better fishin' over that way; anythin's gotta be better than what we bin doin' here all mornin'. Besides, with the weather that's a-comin,' we're soon gonna have to head back that way anyway."

They agreed to haul up their gear and slowly head to the northeast.

Reggie was satisfied of his success as he watched the fishing vessel take the course that would bring the three men into contact with Katie's skiff. Reggie changed course toward the coast, and hopefully toward a late breakfast, brunch, lunch or whatever, because his stomach was beginning to think that his throat had been cut.

Eventually one of the men spotted the old skiff. "What's that dead ahead?" he said.

"Looks like an old life raft," replied another. Then they observed Ms. Katie.

"Now, what have we got here?" said one.

"Looks like a cougar to me," replied the bald headed one.

"C'mon Bobby Jo, be reasonable, how'd a cougar ever get way out here? It's prob'ly just some poor soul's well-fed domestic fat cat."

Ms. Katie, filled with trepidation on their approach, was now giving the vessel her undivided attention. As the men closed on her skiff she twitched her long tail, a typical feline behavior.

"See that!" cried Bobby Jo. "Tolt ya that was a cougar, no domestic cat, not even a feral one got a tail like that!" They gawked in awe with open mouths for several minutes. They were speechless.

Finally one asked, "Wad y'all s'pose we ought a do now?"

"Well, we caint just turn around and leave her way out here," replied another.

"How far are we from shore?" asked Bobby Jo.

"'Bout three miles, more or less," was the considered reply.

"How fast d'y'all all s'pose we could tow that old derelict," Bobby Jo continued.

"Couple of knots at least; take 'bout an hour or so," was the reply.

"Why Bobby Jo, you gonna volunteer to just sashay on over there, reach over the gunnel, and try to find somthin' ta tie a tow rope on to?" another asked.

"Well, not exactly," replied Bobby Jo, as he promptly disappeared below into the cuddy.

A few moments later Bobby Jo reappeared on the open aft deck. The fishing vessel had now drifted to within about 20 or 25 yards of the skiff. Bobby Jo immediately assessed the situation and, with a big, confident smile, said, "Great, fellas, I can do this."

The others watched in silence as he sat down with his favorite bait casting rig on his lap. This cherished old Abu Garcia combo outfit consisted of his prized, Ambassador 7000 bait-casting real mounted on a matched 8-foot graphite composite rod. With the 40-pound Spectra braided line, Bobby Jo could place a cast with remarkable accuracy. He reached way down into his tackle box and retrieved an old 12-ounce lead weight. He placed this weight into a piece of wiping rag and tied it off securely to the end of his line.

Bobby Jo stood, with rod in hand, swinging the weighted piece of rag back and forth testing the feel of it. Then, with a big grin, filled with confidence, Bobby Jo placed a perfect cast, landing the contrived weight just over the near gunnel. They all heard it land with a splash into the bilge of the old derelict skiff.

"Now," said Bobby Jo, "would one of ya old podners care to crank up the li'l old kicker there and head us all ta shore? Easy at first 'till I get my drag set, don't wanna lose 'er to any sudden jerk."

Ms. Katie was terrified! She had never felt so vulnerable and out of control. *Who were these men? What were they going to do to her? Would she be denied a peaceful ending? What had happened to Reggie?* Her imagination ran wild.

She heard the little outboard motor start and saw the sports fishing boat begin to move away from her. A very brief wave of relief washed over her but it was gone in seconds as she noticed that her little lifeboat was beginning to follow along behind the men.

Oh, poop darn! Where are they taking me? What is going on? And where is Reggie?

Ms. Katie had very few firsthand encounters with humans. She inherently feared them and had always observed them from safe cover and distance. She had never considered her fear but simply accepted it. Her fear was like her feelings for the big grizzly bears; she did not know any of them personally either, only about them. In fact, it occurred to Katie that she knew more about the tools and machinery of humans than any of them as individuals. And some of their machinery made a lot of noise and great messes on the land. She always sought Reggie's council to help her reconcile the actions of the machines with the actions of the humans; were they one and the same?

As Reggie had earlier pointed out, if a critter gave it any thought at all, acceptance of life with grace, humility, and dignity is the only truly sustainable alternative. There is a form of peace in acceptance. Until now, she had simply accepted the humans. Reggie had also mentioned that there are no villains or victims in the world of the critters. Life is all about survival.

What is this all about? Katie wondered. *Is this a matter of survival to these men? Are they having visions of a grand feast, of tender princess of cougar roasting on a spit over a roaring beach fire? Will the wolves and others be patiently awaiting their turns for leftovers?*

What is going on this morning? Is this behavior of the marine machine and/or the humans aboard actually saving her?

This would be an act of benevolence not destruction. This did not fit with all the previous observations and experiences she had encountered. All Ms. Katie had seen up until now was the damage and destruction wrought upon her home territory. These wide and seemingly endless corridors, these devastating disruptions to river and stream flows, and these enormous clearings were very troubling to Ms. Katie. They are so intrusive and ominous. They are threatening the very existence—the ultimate survival—of us all.

Is the dark spirit or force causing this? Is it coming from the incredible machines, the detestable human critters, or some combination of them?

After a couple of hours of this mental anguish, Ms. Katie noticed shore for the first time. What a relief. She had finally recovered her sense of direction. Along with this great revelation, she spotted the soaring silhouette of her old pal.

"Oh, how I need you now, Reggie," she said. But she knew he would have to keep his distance from these men.

Then, amazingly, as if on command, a sort of telepathic connection was made. Reggie's image reminded her of another message from earlier: "Breathe, embrace, and believe, Katie!"

"That's it!" she cried aloud. "I've got it! I'm not done yet!"

She would get control of her emotions. She would embrace the moment. She would have a vision of her own, of her freedom. She bet that these men had never had a firsthand encounter with a real wildcat. Incredibly powerful chemicals or feelings were coursing through her body. As her every muscle tensed, so grew her belief in her freedom. Furthermore, Ms. Katie believed that she would meet again with Reggie and they would revisit this part of her life's great journey in every detail.

The three fishermen had chosen a very small shallow pocket cove to disconnect with the old derelict skiff. They had rehearsed their roles so that as the vessels slowed on entering the shallows they could simultaneously cut their fishing/towline and get their boat turned around and away from shore. They were acutely aware how agitated the big cat was and the great threat that she was to their safety. The tillerman was right on cue and the man on the bow was watching for any uncharted rocks.

At the last possible moment Bobby Jo gave the word, cut his line, and the plan unfolded like clockwork. The men were so busy with their tasks that none of them actually saw Katie hit the water. Her long powerful hind legs propelled her up off the shallow sandy bottom and through a rapid series of leaps and bounds on a b-line to shore and the cover of dense salal bushes. The ordeal was over as quickly as it had begun, at least superficially.

With great pride, Reggie circled overhead as the high-pitched whine of the big engine propelled the relieved fishermen up the coast and out of sight.

With the roar of the noisy marine machine ringing in her ears and powerful hormones still flooding her finely tuned body, Ms. Katie rapidly emerged from the dense shoreline brush into the open forest. And, as all terrified felines are wont to do, she ran up the first large fir tree that she came to and took refuge on a large branch about 50 feet above the forest floor. *Safety at last*, she thought, as she gradually regained her composure.

Yet, her continuing conundrum was further confounded by her mixed up emotions. She had been in fear for her very survival. It was this *not knowing of the thing* that had been the source of her fear—no, terror—of becoming a roast dinner for them! But, in hindsight, she realized that these men had only tried to save her! There was no darkness evident in their souls. Obviously, not all humans were possessed of dark spirits. How could you tell friend from foe?

While Ms. Katie was very grateful to these fishermen, her saviors, she was equally confused about this incomprehensible species of critter. There was so much that she didn't understand. She looked forward to her next chance meeting with Reggie with hopes of better fathoming this quandary of contradictions.

But for now, she needed to put some more distance between her and the shoreline. She also needed sleep and food, in no particular order, which ever presented first.
She had survived.

Ms. Katie Cougar
and the Old Lady

Bobby and Ollie had been foraging and scavenging all morning along a stretch of shallow sand beach, then below some high bluffs, and then onto another pebble beach. Their efforts, as happened so often, were richly rewarded. Their tummies were quite comfortable, and they were nearing their midday rest time.

Ollie was off on another dive, and Bobby had paused to peruse her surroundings, especially using her super-sensitive nose. This particular area was just on the outskirts of a human settlement. Although this pebble beach was seldom used much by the humans, all concerned tended to respect one another and kept their distances.

This stretch of the coast was fully exposed to the big straight, but fortunately it was not exposed to the Great Ocean, as it was protected by the snow peaked mountainous peninsula on the opposite shore. And what a magnificent scenic backdrop those white topped mountains made.

Interestingly, this vast section of water, this strait, was reputed to be the only connection for several hundreds of miles up the coast between the expansive inland sea and the Great Ocean, the Mother of all seas. And the huge inland sea consisted of many other expansive sections of water all interconnected. This sweep of shoreline is close enough to the place where the Great Ocean tides begin their floods and ebbs, at times enduring formidable currents and winds, and the never-ending ocean swells. Bobby's ancestors had long believed that the waters that flooded and ebbed through here were rich in nutrients because all species of critters thrived here.

In fact, according to the old tales of Bobby's elders, as related by her mother, the ancestral humans had a name for the great inland body of water: the Salish Sea. Furthermore, they collectively referred to themselves as the Coast Salish peoples. Bobby's elders believed that these humans had many large settlements, with even larger territories, widely dispersed throughout their Salish Sea. They explained that the continuing increases in these humans was the same as for all the other animals: the abundance of food and other necessities for life. With the exception of a few of the whales returning with young from their long winter journeys south without food, and the occasional diseases and pestilences, starvation was very rare.

Ollie surfaced, and after chewing noisily and swallowing some scrumptious morsel, he said "Hey Bobby, did I catch you day dreaming? There are lots of juicy mud worms here. I've almost has as much food as I'll need; one more dive and I'll join you for our midday rest." And with a flip of his long, tapered tail he disappeared once more below the surface.

Bobby, seeing a couple of promising logs among the driftwood just below overhanging bushes at the forest edge, ambled over to see if she could roll one of them over. After all, this scavenging strategy had been quite productive most of the morning. These logs had probably been deposited far above the normal summer high tide line during one of last winter's storms. Only a critter with her great strength could roll some of these logs over to reap the ripe rewards exposed.

Bobby, as usual, was totally engrossed in her business. A voice startled her: "Well, how do you do, Bobby?"

The great bear reared up in surprise and, shaking her head from side to side, up and down, she caught sight of Ms. Katie, high above her in an Arbutus tree.

"Why did you do that?" growled Bobby. "You made my old heart skip a bunch of beats. Couldn't you have moved, or rustled some leaves, or made a less shocking pronouncement of your presence? You do annoy me so when you do that you know!"

On surfacing, Ollie, surprised, quickly got the gist of the situation. He immediately re-submerged and headed back toward the sand beach. He'd catch up with Bobby later.

"I'm sincerely sorry that I have upset you, Bobby, I do hope you'll forgive me," implored Katie.
With that, the easy going, mild mannered Bobby was instantly appeased. "Okay Ms. Katie, you sneaky old devil, how could I ever be angry with you for even a moment or two?"

"Bobby, as you probably know," said Katie, "one of the greatest gifts we cougars receive as kittens is the gift of stealth—to be sneaky, as you say. We learn it in play. We learn to move using almost all of our muscles, with total concentration, very slowly, very deliberately, so that our motion is barely noticeable.

"We also learn to be very still, motion-less, often for very long periods. Absolutely still and quiet." continued Katie.

"Once mastered, it is a fascinating experience. The world carries on, oblivious to our presence. Our state of awareness is dramatically enhanced. It is very rewarding and fulfilling, especially for our tummies. Many of my meals come to me on their own four legs." Katie said with a smile.

"But alas, this ingrained skill of stealth, like having a magic cloak, does have this downside, as I did seriously disturb your concentration, upsetting you. And again my dear friend Bobby, I am very sorry," pleaded Ms. Katie.

"Well thank you Katie, I do understand, and I have fully recovered my composure. I also appreciate the great advantage it is for you cougars to sneak around so," replied Bobby. "Since most of my meals are found under rocks or logs, washed up on shore, growing on berry bushes, or swimming in streams or rivers almost under my nose, there is no need for me to sneak up on them. Besides, growing up as cubs our play focused on very different skill sets, like running, climbing, and tussling," Bobby explained.

"I understand where you are coming from, Bobby," said Katie, "and I certainly respect your great strength and stamina, especially the power of your paws, and the ferocity of your claws. Forbid that I should ever feel the bite of your jaws. I respect your bravery, too.

"You are a dear friend and ally, Bobby. Our bantering just reminded me of an interesting incident that happened to me a few years ago in this very area, a little farther along where one of the farms comes almost right down to the shore.

"As you have no doubt experienced, Bobby, in the fall, as the apples are ripening, the deer congregate in the orchards. And, as you like a good feed of fallen apples, I also enjoy a good feed of fresh venison.

"It was a fine fall day. This farm in particular had an apple orchard that was adjacent to this pebble beach. I was at the edge of the bank overlooking a narrow stretch of the beach, crouched in the dense shade of the trees and salal bushes. In my manner, invisible and undetectable. My magic cloak was working.

"A human appeared, walking along the beach directly toward me. She was an old female. She was steeply stooped over and seemed intently focused on her feet. It was a very interesting and puzzling behavior to observe. *What was she looking for?* I wondered.

"Then, along came another human. This one was a very young male. He was riding a very large bicycle along the farm lane leading to the beach. At the end of the lane, the young boy dismounted from his bicycle and began watching the elderly woman, too. She continued with this rather odd behavior, slowly plodding along, looking at her feet in total concentration. *What was she doing?*

"After a while, the boy broke his stillness and silence and approached the old lady. They walked along together, the boy apparently mimicking her odd behavior.

I was so still, I could hear my heartbeat slowly thumping in my ears. I could also hear every word they were speaking as they were so close to me. They were almost directly below me, and totally oblivious to me, just as you had been earlier here," explained Katie.

"The old lady said to the young boy, 'I'm looking for agates. Have you ever seen an agate, young Kimmie?'

"Then they sat on a huge drift log immediately under my nose. I picked up a strong scent of perfume coming from the old lady. The boy just smelled like boy," said Katie.

"The boy seemed intent on what she was about to show him. From among the folds of her clothing she retrieved a small pouch. From this pouch she shook out several pebbles into her hand and displayed them for young Kimmie," Katie explained.

'Wow!' exclaimed Kimmie.

"I almost gasped in utter amazement too, Bobby, these were not like ordinary pebbles, not like any that I had ever seen. Why Bobby, the sun struck one of them and it seemed almost alive. It was as if it was filled with energy. It seemed to almost glow. The boy picked up this pebble from her hand and studied it, also in obvious awe and amazement.

'It is beautiful,' he said. 'May I help you with your search?'

"With that, they slowly resumed their interesting behavior, plodding farther on up the beach.

"As I watched them recede and saw them examine a few more pebbles I pondered their relationship. Could they have a kinship or dependency? The boy seemed so young and she so old. Yet, they seemed to enjoy a bond of peace and trust.

"And what was their most unusual behavior about? Surely pebbles had no nutritional value. What could this apparent searching have to do with survival or protection? Could certain pebbles contain some other form of energy or power? Regardless, these humans were certainly very interesting individuals, neither seeming to be any threat to me.

"So there I crouched, for perhaps another hour or more, watching and listening as the world moved on," concluded Ms. Katie.

"That was a heartwarming and intriguing tale, Katie, thank you." said Bobby. "It may comfort you to know that the many questions that you conclude with are eerily similar to the many questions that continue to perplex me. These humans truly are an enigma. These mysterious pebbles seem like just another piece of the puzzle."

"So it seems," said Ms. Katie.

"I've wondered, Katie, if someday one of us might be able to connect with one of these humans sufficiently to establish a rapport," queried Bobby.

"You may be on to something there, my dear optimistic friend," said Ms. Katie. "Perhaps we ought to keep an eye on that young one the old lady called Kimmie. He may be our best bet."

"Agreed," replied Bobby. "Interestingly, I think I may have encountered that young Kimmie before. Also, we should consult Reggie the next time one of us happens upon him. He's sure to have timely and sage advice."

"I agree, too," said Ms. Katie. "And, thank you Bobby, for this has been a fortuitous meeting, although it got off to a rough start with me startling you," she said with an impish grin. As I was about to lower my magic cloak and quit this place moments before you came, it's time now for me to be moving on."

"Understood, Katie," said Bobby. "Besides, I'm almost at a favorite resting spot, and it won't be long before Ollie comes along. He always does, eventually, bless his restless soul. Take care, Katie."

Who's There? ...
The Knowing of It.

One late fall afternoon Bobby and Ollie retreated from a successful morning of foraging along this long spit. The wind came up and they sought shelter for their rest period in the quiet lee of the inside shore.

As they settled in for their afternoon rest, Bobby asked Ollie, "Do you remember the time when we happened upon Ms. Katie awhile back, when she gave me such an awful scare? Well, I've been thinking of that time. I've been trying to figure out how it had happened that I had not known that she was there. And I think I've got it, Ollie. It was because of you, Ollie."

"Me! Why me?" cried Ollie.

"No, no," implored Bobby, "I didn't mean *because of you* in a negative or bad way. I meant that it had been because of the security and comfort that I feel being with you. Let me explain. If I had been alone I very likely would have known that someone was watching me. I would have sensed it. Do you understand what I'm trying to say, Ollie? Please help me; oh this is difficult to explain."

"I'm not sure that I do understand, Bobby," ventured Ollie, "but I am listening to you. I am trying my best. Please do go on."

"Well Ollie," continued Bobby. "I believe that it all has to do with the knowing of a thing. Let me start by telling you what it is not. It is not like knowing about a thing by its smell, or because we can see it with our own eyes. It is not because of how it feels, like a sudden drop in temperature, or how it sounds, like the wind and the waves right now, or the waterfalls at the head of the lagoon."

"Oh, I think I'm starting to get it," replied Ollie enthusiastically. "Do you mean something like how we know about a big storm several hours before it gets here? It's the early knowing of the thing that lets us get to high ground or safe shelter before the thing happens? Is that what you are trying to share Bobby?"

"Well, sort of. But not quite." Bobby patiently persisted. "The *knowing* that I'm trying to explain is much more in the present, and perhaps very close, right here and right now. And this *knowing* of the thing is an especially powerful feeling when we're alone."

"Yes, yes Bobby! Now I know what you are talking about," exclaimed Ollie with excitement and relief. "It's the feeling that I get, the sure *knowing* of it when someone is watching me. Who's there? Come out, come out, whoever you are. I know you're there. Even if, like Ms. Katie, the *whoever* may not have meant me any harm, I just know I'm being watched."

"Yes, you've got it, Ollie!" cried Bobby elatedly. "The *knowing of it*, although you can't smell it, see it, taste it, hear it, or even touch it. You just know it's there; somewhere very close. It makes the hair stand up on the back of my neck sometimes. That was difficult for me to express, Ollie. Thank you for your patience."

"But now that we are there, and together with this understanding, I want to share with you a most amazing event that I witnessed quite a while ago," said Bobby. "It was the alarming meeting with Ms. Katie recently that triggered the memory of this encounter.

"I was alone at the time," began Bobby, "my memory is very clear. In fact, we were all alone when it started. And none of us, at least none of the others, I believed initially, were aware that they were not alone."

"Hold up there Bobby," asked Ollie, "don't lose me now. Back up, please. Who are they? And where were all of you?"

"Sorry Ollie," said Bobby, "this is such a difficult event to describe, I just wanted to get it all out, afraid I'd lose the memory. Let me start over. I had been living in this large inlet farther up the coast. There are many islands in this inlet, and quite a few of them are an easy swim from shore. This particular island that I had been on was only a very short swim from the big shore. The long deep channel between the island and the shore would normally only take about 15 minutes to cross. I say normally because there are times—in fact, two times a day— when it is not possible to cross because of the current. The water flows so swiftly through this channel, first one direction, then the other. It flows as swiftly as the big rivers in the fall after the rains when the salmon come back to spawn."

"Wow, I get the picture, Bobby," offered Ollie. "That is a powerful force of water. The kind of currents that I like to play in, but I'll save that thought for another time. So, there you are on the island, headed back to the big shore."

"Yes Ollie, thank you," replied Bobby. "But as I watched I could see that the current was still too strong for me to swim across, and I would have to wait for the slack tide. It was while I was laying and waiting that I noticed the others on the big shore side."

"Slow down again please, Bobby," appealed Ollie. "Let me keep up with you. These others, how many were there? Who were they?"

"I'm sorry, Ollie," said Bobby, "sharing this story is such a challenge. It happened so quickly. And I can't tell it in the manner of how it smelled or sounded; it's all about this *knowing* of things."

After a pause to ponder, Bobby continued. "Well, there were only two other beings. The first one that I noticed was a man slowly walking along the pebble beach as if he were searching for something. He stopped a couple of times and looked up and around, all around, even behind and up at the sky. Then he resumed his search. I did not notice the other for a while. In fact, I had no idea that there was another until the man suddenly stopped again. This time he did not look all around, he simply stood motionless, staring straight ahead.

"I shifted my focus and started looking very closely at the shoreline and the bushes just above the low bank ahead of the man. I focused intently on a spot in the direction that the man seemed to be staring at. Then I sensed it, too. I even thought I saw eyes. But there was nothing physically identifiable there. Just the powerful presence of it, Ollie. It was almost exactly like the situation when I happened upon Ms. Katie when she almost frightened the life out of me."

"You mean you saw a cougar, Bobby?" inquired Ollie.

"Yes…no…well, sort of," stammered Bobby. "Ollie, as I've been trying to tell you, I could not see this thing, whoever, whatever. I just knew it was there. There was a tremendous force present in those salal bushes just above the beach. A muscular force, waiting, ready to spring into devastating action. I just *knew* the presence of that force that was waiting, silent, motionless, and invisible."

"I'm with you Bobby," encouraged Ollie. "I understand. Why that could actually have been Ms. Katie hiding in those salal bushes."

"Yes, but not at all likely Ollie," replied Bobby, "because this place is many days and several territories north of here. And besides, she's always had it way too good down here to have ever contemplated moving. Although, it might have been a relative of hers."

"Wow, so what happened next?" prompted Ollie.

"I shifted my focus back to the man," continued Bobby. "He was still standing there, motionless, and staring in the direction of that force. What was so amazing was I could see that from his angle, he could not possibly have seen the thing. He had to have been sensing it, knowing it, just like me. But then I noticed something else. Something very powerful, an emotional tension was coming from the man. And I recognized what it was right away. It was fear. I knew it was fear coming from him.

"And, right at that moment, Ollie, I realized that the hidden whoever, whatever, *knew* it, too. The tremendous energy, the muscular force pent up in those salal bushes, increased noticeably, as if in response to sensing the fear.

"Also in that same moment, more amazing things happened. The man removed a dark object from his pocket, manipulated it, and a long, shiny, silvery object appeared in his hand. Then he pulled an orange object from his other pocket. He appeared to open it, looked at it for a moment, then closed it, and just held it in his fist.

"Then two of the most incredible things happened, Ollie. At the very moment that the man, just standing there, the long silvery object in one hand, the orange object in his other hand, looked up and stared in the direction of the invisible entity, his fear went away. Yes, it dissipated like the morning mists before the rising sun. All gone. No more fear.

"Equally astounding, Ollie, the tremendously powerful force of energy that had been coming from the salal bushes had begun dissipating too. I just *knew*, I could sense the tension in the muscles of the thing beginning to relax. I just *knew* these things, Ollie. That's what's made the telling of this so very hard."

"I understand, Bobby," consoled Ollie, "but please don't stop now, Bobby. Please go on. What happened next?"

"Well, as I said," continued Bobby, "this amazing experience happened so quickly, it was over in minutes. The man slowly started backing up, then he stopped. Then he slowly backed up some more, all the while with the objects in his hands, and continuing to stare in the direction of the salal bushes. Finally, he turned around, and very slowly walked back along the beach, only stopping occasionally to look up and all around. I continued watching him until he walked around a point and out of sight."

"And what about the invisible entity?" inquired Ollie.

"By then the great force of energy in the salal bushes had dissipated to nothing," informed Bobby. "I couldn't even imagine eyes or any forms in the shadows. It was as if it had never been."

"Do you suppose, Bobby, that either of the others were aware of you?" Ollie asked.

"I've thought about that too, Ollie," answered Bobby. "I'm fairly certain that the invisible one had likely been there before I came to the channel to check the flow of the water. This one was likely watching me as I looked for a place to lie down to await the slack tide.

"But, as for the man, I'm also fairly certain that he did not know of my presence. Firstly, I was already lying down when he came along. Secondly, he would never have known of any danger from me because there never was any; I was too far away across the channel.

"For all our world's knowledge, Ollie," concluded Bobby, "it would appear that nothing had ever happened that day. That I had simply imagined the whole of it."

"But," added Ollie, "as I was listening to you, I was thinking of the man on the beach. That part of your story amazed me the most. It has been my experience that few humans seem to have the ability to *know* about things as we do. As humans go, this man's perception is remarkable."

"True, Ollie," said Bobby. "I too have seen many humans, closer to their home territories, walk right by me looking down at little objects in their hands, never paying me any mind. As the years go by, they seem to be losing their awareness of the world around them. Their behavior is most puzzling. But remember, Ollie, this man was alone and very far from the safety of his home. This may have enhanced his perception."

"Understood, Bobby," continued Ollie. "What do you suppose those objects were, the shiny one and the orange one, that the man used? It seems that they had great powers for the man, that they took away his fear!"

"These are great comments, Ollie," said Bobby. "These humans truly are an enigma. But, like other great mysteries we have pondered and resolved, we will figure these out, too, another day. I'm getting hungry; it's time for us to go foraging again."

Reggie's 50 Shades of Green

As was the pattern of most of their days these past gorgeous weeks, Bobby and Ollie scoured the rocky shoreline interspersed with pebble and sand beaches seeking food, fun, or adventure, in no particular order. Bobby by land and Ollie by sea, they paralleled each other as they progressed along the coast where the forest and the ocean meet.

This intriguing and productive boundary between worlds is always changing, with the most frequent changes amongst the tides. Each flood brings fresh surprises, and each ebb exposes tidal pools and freshly replenished delicacies in cracks and crevasses, and spaces beneath and between rocks. This intertidal area also changes with the weather—especially during and following storms—and with the seasons. In the late fall and early winter, the dieback of the kelp plants is evident, but it grows back rapidly in the spring. Bull kelp is the fastest growing seaweed in the world. It can grow from a tiny spore into a 200 foot long plant in one summer!

"Look what I've picked up!" cried Ollie. He had just surfaced from the depths of a bull kelp forest and was dragging a delicious starry flounder ashore to share with Bobby.

"Wonderful," replied Bobby, "but I've been feasting on the remains of this white-sided dolphin that I found. So, Ollie, thanks, but your catch is all yours. We have all we'll need for a while."

As they proceeded along the beach on this beautiful September day, the adventurous pair arrived at a particularly narrow stretch. The beach was so narrow that in one spot an ancient contorted arbutus tree arched completely over the beach with lower branches reaching precariously out over the water.

"Ah ha!" proclaimed Bobby, "our midday rest spot has just presented itself. My, what a wonderful world."

"Agree," replied Ollie as he looked up, "And look who's already here."

A familiar high pitched squeaking, squawking, chirping voice came from high in the ancient arbutus above.

Ollie smiled because ordinarily such a high pitched voice might be associated with a small shorebird such as a plover, a curlew, or even a passing pair of bright red beaked oystercatchers. Anyone unfamiliar would never believe that such a large, majestic, and imposing bird such as the bald eagle could have such an un-majestic voice. But few, even the uninitiated, would be so foolish as to comment on it, especially in the presence of Reginald Regal Eagle I.

"Well hello Reggie, long time no see," said Ollie in his swift manner of speech.

"Well hello to the pair of you, too," replied Reggie, "and welcome to my favorite roost along here. How have you been fairing?"

"Bobby and I have been enjoying each other's company, and have fed well today thanks, Reggie," said Ollie. "Bobby had just commented what a wonderful world this is, as we were arriving. What have you been up to?"

"I'm very happy to say that I too have been dining very well; the rivers are running heavy with spawning salmon," Reggie shared. "And today I have simply enjoyed soaring on the powerful warm air currents high over our bountiful island rainforests. My how the trees grow! I came to the cool air along this beach to rest and contemplate the beauty of our wonderful world. I have especially been pondering the many shades of green on the slopes, and how they seem to be ever changing. Why, one slope I remember well had been a deep rich dark green last year. I had fed well on the big red-backed salmon in the stream below. And earlier today I discovered that there was very little green there at all. In fact, almost all the trees are gone."

"All gone, you say?" said Bobby. "And what of the salmon? They are on my menu right now, too."

"Well Bobby," replied Reggie, "I was way too high, and the angle of the light was not right for seeing into the water. Besides, I was more focused on all the tree stumps, and the red tree branches everywhere on the ground. I also noted that a few hawks were feeding very well on the many small mice and moles that no longer had the cover of the trees and shrubs."

"I see what you mean by 'ever-changing,' Reggie," said Ollie, "and that's a pretty dramatic change. Although, perhaps in a couple of years Bobby will be able to go up into that valley and feast on fresh crops of sweet berries."

"Yes," said Reggie, "I've seen it before too, but often the thriving berry bushes seem to die off suddenly, only to be replaced by yet another shade of green, a very much lighter shade of the green of younger trees. And over time, it seems that more and more of the slopes of our island are covered with varying shades of green from the light, lustrous, vibrant shades to the rich, dark, and sometimes dull shades. But there are still a few places, especially along the high slopes, that have yet another distinct shade; this is a more pale gray-green. Also, there are more gray skeletons of trees scattered around. The old skeletons make great roosts for me, particularly where they are near streams or lakes. The woodpeckers fare well on those old relics, too. Their persistent pecking and hammering often echoes up the valleys."

"I remember wandering up such a gray-green valley once," commented Bobby. "I clearly remember all the big turkey vultures slowly circling overhead. It seems that they can smell a meal a mile away. And, sure enough, they eventually lead me to a delicious, recently deceased cow elk. I recall, they weren't very friendly; they did a lot of hissing and grunting, which I quickly came to understand is all the voice that they've got. I figured they were just protesting me interrupting their meal. But I only stayed for one serving of that scrumptious meat and moved on up the valley for the night."

"Listening to you, Reggie, has triggered memories of shades of green for me too," added Ollie. "Every spring I've noticed the increasing sunlight and warmth brings out new pale green shoots from the ends of the branches of the coniferous or evergreen trees. My eyes have often been attracted to the remarkable two-toned color scheme contrasting the light pale green of the new needles with the much darker green of the older needles. Also, even changing light conditions bring about changes in shades of green. Why just look down there at the beautiful bull kelp blades being left behind on the beach by the ebb tide. See how the sunlight from offshore is causing fascinating iridescent shades of green in the kelp leaves. The surfaces of those wet leaves almost seem to shimmer. I'd bet that if we watched as the light of day changes, we'll see at least 50 shades of green right there."

"But now that you've got me going Reggie," continued Ollie, "I'd like to offer a marine perspective on shades of green. As you know, I spend much of my life on and beneath our emerald sea. The spring and summer bring about the most dramatic changes, especially as the marine plants, mostly kelps, are almost finished growing; the waters become very green. At the peak of the kelp blooms, the water can be such a thick green that I can't see anything. Fortunately, there are a few muddy silty areas, because at least there I can feel around and usually manage to find enough mud worms to get me by. But often I may have to travel several miles to find clear water. And thankfully, I can often dig up a few clams along the beaches."

"That's true on land too," commented Bobby. "I've also seen the colored powders fall from the plants and trees in the spring, and I've seen this completely change the colors of freshwater ponds, pools, and lakes, just as you have described. Although there are other colors than green, such as yellows and whites."

"I agree," supported Ollie. "Once, I even encountered a stretch of water off a particular beach that was a deep rusty red from the surface to the bottom. And I believe—even

Reggie will agree—that in all its shades, it is a wonderful world."

And with that, Bobby was nodding off, Reggie had gone silent, and Ollie stretched, rolled over, and drifted off to sleep, too. The sounds of the waves gently lapping on the beach pebbles, and the sea breeze softly swishing through the evergreen arbutus leaves carried the three characters off to their Land of Nod.

Reggie's Reincarnation

For many of the critters along the northeast coast of the Great Ocean, winters are quite dull and dreary times, with the exception, of course, of those who hibernate. Following the fall equinox, the days get progressively shorter and the nights longer until the arrival of the solstice. And even after the solstice, it can seem to take forever for the temporal pattern to begin a noticeable reversal. Temperatures decrease night and day, often plummeting quite dramatically during the early morning hours. The winter storms rolling in off the Great Ocean often arrive as a succession of powerful disturbances, one after another. Their impact along the shores can be devastatingly brutal and punishing. These storms are invariably packing great quantities of moisture collected from the surface of the sea. The coastal areas are frequently pummeled by great deluges of rain. And as this moisture-laden air is driven farther inland to higher elevations by the raging winds, the precipitation manifests as snow—appreciable amounts of it.

These dull dreary times can be very hard on the critters, especially the elderly, infirm, or injured. Oftentimes, this will be when the body, mind, and souls simply give up and part company.

But sometimes the universe can show considerable kindness and compassion right in the midst of all this dullness and dreariness. Many of the living things consider such periods of grace as mid-winter's reprieves. But, such times of magnanimity are never a guarantee. We have all, at some time, experienced a hard winter without this courtesy. Therefore, when critters sense the onset of a mid-winter's reprieve, it is a time to get out and about, a time to enjoy and rejoice.

It was just before the solstice when the winds went calm, the skies became clear bright blue, and the temperatures soared, that two of our favorite characters, Bobby the big black bear and Ollie the recalcitrant adolescent river otter, emerged from their winter shelters. They were ecstatic!

Bobby came out of her den first into the glorious warmth of the mid-winter morning sun. After much stretching, scratching and rolling about, Bobby set out for the shore not far below her secluded sanctuary. She had two expectations: she hoped to scrounge around the boulders and find a few juicy tender morsels to appease her ravenous appetite; and she also knew that her pal, Ollie, would likely soon be popping out of one of the rocky crevasses nearby. Her optimism was soon to be rewarded.

Ollie was deep in the back of a fissure in an outcrop of rock not far above the high waterline. Interestingly, his delightful reverie was rudely interrupted by a young mink. This ambitious little fellow had been up and about for an hour or more enjoying the unseasonably mild spell. He was systematically searching every crack and cranny he came upon in the hopes of securing a meal when he suddenly stumbled upon Ollie. Had anyone been watching it would have been hard to tell which of the two had been more surprised. The outcome of the encounter could have been tragic for the mink had Ollie not been so lethargically impaired. By the time Ollie had fully recovered his faculties and wits, the nimble little mink was probably half a mile away.

Ollie crawled out of his shelter onto the rocky outcrop, which afforded him a commanding perspective; he could see almost the entire big bay. His thoughts turned to Bobby. He visually searched for her. His surveillance was soon successful. She appeared to have just rolled over a substantial bolder in her search for sustenance. Ollie set off to join her.

Ollie's rapid movements as he bounded along caught Bobby's attention and she invited her dear friend to share in the bounties of her good fortune. As they merrily munched away they agreed that this was definitely a time to enjoy and rejoice. One never knew how long a mid-winter's reprieve might last. Amazingly, they both came up with the idea to seek an adventure at their beloved soft sand beach just beyond the rocky headland to the west of the entrance of their big bay. After cleaning up their spoils and feeling quite refreshed and reinvigorated they set off in high spirits.

Along the way, Ollie told Bobby of the rude awakening from the impertinent little mink. "He roused me from the reverie I was enjoying in the recesses of my favorite crevasse! You know, Bobby, someday that little fellow's luck will run out, and I hope that I'll be there to savor the moment."

Bobby replied, "Yes Ollie, this unseasonably mild weather has obviously summoned all but the true hibernators and there probably will be no solitude to be found for the duration of this warm spell. Why I believe I even saw old Reggie soaring above the treetops near the back of the bay when I first gazed about. During winter's worst weather eagles will seek the security of sheltered roosts, but they're sure to be very active now, too."

"That may add even more excitement to our adventure," commented Ollie as they continued silently along the well-defined trail headed toward their favorite soft sand beach.

While the belligerent birds were setting up for their ambush formation high in the coniferous canopy of the point of land, totally unknown to them, Reggie was rapidly approaching a horrific misadventure.

Reggie had indeed left the forested shoreline near the back of the big sheltered bay and had begun winging his way over the expanse of water toward the wide entrance to the bay. He intended to move his search for a meal to the beautiful beach just outside and to the west of the bay. It was often a very productive place and he felt a slight twinge of excitement.

Then Reggie made a monumental mistake! As he was exiting the bay, without any apparent logic, rhyme, or reason, he went into a glide and added a slight side-slip to the configuration of his body and wings. This horizontal angling facilitates a loss of altitude without the usual increase in speed. But, whatever reason he may have had for setting up a low and slow glide around the rocky headland no one will ever know. He rounded the point level with the height of the rocks with a clear view beneath the canopy of the majestic mature Douglas fir, spruce, and hemlock trees.

He was totally oblivious to the peril that awaited above him. A marauding murder of crows perched in seclusion in the high crowns of those same evergreen trees was locked and loaded. And ready to kill.

As Reggie passed below them, they exploded from their lofty perches. They immediately had the decided advantage of their surprise attack from above. Their much shorter narrower wings afforded them far superior speed and maneuverability than their prodigious prey. And the big raptor was gliding so slowly!

Within minutes Reggie had sustained several punishing body blows, was losing what little altitude he had and was gasping for air. The coup de grâce came as a paralyzing stab to the base of his skull. Reggie lost consciousness in that instant and never felt the impact with the ground. Neither had he seen his two old friends ambling along one of the trails approaching the beach.

Bobby had just realized that the tree canopy cover overhead had broken, clear sky and the beach were directly ahead beyond the brush cover. Momentarily, as bears are frequently want to do, she reared up on her hind legs to peek over the salal bordering the beach to see if the way was safe. She immediately noticed this murder of crows doing their victory dance hopping around their fallen feathery prey. Bobby's instinct compelled her to seize the moment. She broke cover and bounded down onto the beach. With Ollie hot on her heals the crows immediately took flight and relinquished their great prize.

Ollie was the first to recognize the mass of feathers as he stammered in confusion and disbelief, "Why Bobby, this is Reggie!"

Bobby was stuck for several moments in total denial. "Are you sure? How could this have happened?"

They were in shock!

One of Reggie's wings lay at an unnatural angle and was obviously broken. Bobby cautiously moved forward and nosed Reggie. When she nudged Reggie's head it flopped over on the sand as if it were only attached by the white feather-covered skin of his neck. The sight produced immediate sensations of nausea and revulsion in them.

Ollie moaned, "I can see no signs of life."

Bobby moved back on her haunches, traumatized and deeply disturbed. She said, "At this moment, I have to agree."

A deep pall came over them as the beating of their hearts reverberated in their ears. All was eerily silent as the pain of their loss slowly settled in.

Bobby again moved her giant head forward over Reggie and breathed in deeply. She hovered over Reggie for several more moments and then resumed her contemplative posture on her haunches.

After several more moments of silence, Bobby finally said, "While I have to agree, Ollie, it does appear that there are no visible signs of life, I do detect a distinct sent, or perhaps it is simply a sense of life. Perhaps it is Reggie's soul which has yet to depart his warm limp body."

Reggie looked pretty darn dead!

"You know, Ollie," began Bobby, "eagles, like bears and river otters, have very few natural predators. And old eagles don't get to be old eagles without paying due respect and diligence to the awesome ever-present threat of the murderous crows! This scene defies explanation."

They were in total shock.

Ollie was perplexed. He had never contemplated the philosophical concepts of minds, bodies, and souls; but, neither would he deny the possibilities of their existence. In fact, Ollie had only the most rudimentary concepts of life and death, like day and night, or black and white.

Ollie had the highest respect for Bobby and the seemingly vast repository of knowledge that had been passed down to her from her ancestors over the millennia of generations. Ollie was all ears waiting to hear Bobby's thoughts on their predicament.

Bobby slowly began to share a very tall tale. "According to legend," she said, "powerful healing places exist along our coast. One of these mystical places just happens to be only an hour or so from here. Animals would bring their sick or injured friends to this otherworldly place and leave them to the mercies of the mighty spirits that reside nearby. These great healing spirits determine the final fates of those delivered to them."

Ollie replied, "While I've never heard of such magical healing places, I have encountered a couple of places where I experienced the emergence of immense flows of energy. At one such place, I spread my exhausted worn out body at the base of a giant cedar tree overlooking a creek above a falls, and experienced an unbelievable state of relaxation and received huge surges of restorative energy. This remarkable reinvigoration lasted for many days. I visited one of these places a couple of times. And, I believe there are many other such places."

"Yes," agreed Bobby, "there are many amazing aspects of our world that are just beyond the abilities of our primary senses to detect. But, firstly, there has to be a unity or connectedness of our bodies, minds, and spirits, and secondly, there has to be a receptiveness for us to even detect the presence of such places. When we are in that receptive state, we may even detect advanced warnings of impending dangers.

"So," continued Ollie, "do you think there is anything that we can do for Reggie?"

"Well, we'll never know if we never try," said Bobby. "Further to the legends, not all cases have resulted in successful healing or recoveries, but there have been a few remarkable tales. Sometimes, a healing has taken weeks or months, while the fates of other unfortunate souls, sadly, have remained mysteries."

"Well," said Ollie, "let's get at it."

With his dexterous paws, he gently repositioned Reggie's deformed wing alongside his body and aligned him ready to be moved. Bobby opened her massive muzzle, and while allowing her lips to completely cover her teeth, she gingerly enveloped Reggie's feathery body and slowly picked him up. And off they went.

The mystical healing place was a relatively small unremarkable clearing in the forest. This clearing was adjacent to a long-abandoned meadow. The meadow had once been a part of a much larger and probably very productive farm in its day. Old tractor trails traced the boundaries of other meadows and there was evidence of more recent wheel marks around the adjacent meadow. These wheel marks were not fresh; months old at least from the previous summer or fall. The mid-winter air was still, warm, and calm.

Only the occasional hammering of a nearby woodpecker, perhaps a pileated, interrupted the silence of the mid-winter's afternoon.

Although Ollie's senses were wary and vigilant and he felt fully alert and receptive, he detected nothing. It was just a typical day with the exception that it was an amazingly warm day during a mid-winter's reprieve from the blustery wet and cold winds. It was a day in a place and time that they would never forget.

Bobby placed Reggie in the middle of the healing place and sat nearby in deep meditation. Ollie respectfully, slowly, and quietly joined her. He sat absolutely still and in total silence for what seemed to him an incredibly long time. This was most uncharacteristic behavior for Ollie, the normally hyperactive chatterbox.

In due course, Bobby rose, sniffed the air, and nodded her great head indicating that they were done. They had finished what they had set out to accomplish, now it was time to leave Reggie in the care of the healing spirits and get on with their lives.

Dark and thickening high-altitude clouds built to the west. The wind was cooling and freshening. This was a definite harbinger of the return of their winter and the end of their brief but delightful reprieve. Bobby picked up a trail heading back in the direction of their big sheltered bay where they would likely be holed up for the remaining few weeks of winter and continue savoring their memories of Reggie.

Bobby and Ollie observed similar patterns of movement among several of their fellow critters as they returned to their respective dens, crevasses, and burrows to resume their long winter's naps.

They passed the last weeks of winter in quiet and uneventful solitude.

During the last of Bobby's days in her dark den, she had been dreaming of enjoyable adventures that may lie ahead, especially getting out to a beach.

Now that spring had finally arrived along the northeast coast of the Great Ocean, and the land was full of celebratory song and bountiful bloom, Bobby and Ollie were able to relax and immerse themselves in it. They were thankful that neither the landscape nor the critters living upon it had suffered any significant issues or losses throughout the winter.

"We have a lot to be thankful for, Ollie," said Bobby. "Savor the delightful sights, sounds, and smells of spring. This is my favorite season of the year. The vernal equinox will soon be upon us. Life is very good indeed."

"Yesterday evening, while watching some raccoons foraging on the mudflat behind the little island, I reconnected with a very dear old friend, Miss Effie. Her people, great blue herons, are among the most stealthy and successful fishermen I've ever known. She and hers have fared well this past winter, too, and are anxiously awaiting the return of the herring, and one of the greatest spawning events on this beautiful blue planet. Miss Effie had just chosen another new mate and was getting acquainted with his territory. Our visit was curtailed by her rapidly encroaching masked neighbors, the ravenous raccoons. She left in a flurry with grating, coarse, croaking vocalizations. Sometimes I imagine that her ancestors must have been related to the great flying dinosaurs. At least it is comforting to know that Miss Effie is still active and well."

"That is very funny, Bobby, but you may well be right about Miss Effie's ancestral beginnings. And her comment about the imminent return of the herring reminded me of springs past when I have seen some of the protected waters along our coast turned white like milk when the male herring begin fertilizing the roe. I once even had a taste of that roe; it is delicious! I would have stayed for more, alas, there were too many wolves gorging on the succulent spring special, and I didn't fancy being the last course of their banquet. So, I moved on."

"And I agree that we *do* live in an amazingly bountiful place, this highly productive northeast coast of the Great Ocean. We are truly blessed. But, having said that, Bobby, I must confess that these past few weeks of winter, and since giving up our winter shelters, I have been unable to avoid the persistent memories of Reggie."

"Yes, Ollie, I too have been plagued by the incessant images of Reggie's unfortunate encounter with the murder of crows. I am especially beleaguered by all the unanswered questions. I propose a plan," declared Bobby.

And so it was immediately agreed that they return to their beloved beach, both being of the strong belief that their mystery would be resolved, somehow. So, they set off to return to the scene.

On arrival, almost at the far westerly end of the beach, they spotted a very familiar looking site, a fully mature great bald eagle.

"Could it be?" cried Ollie.

As they stood there in awe, the great bald eagle, with a single flap of his powerful broad wings, launched himself from his perch and glided into the brisk breeze directly toward them. With total trust and confidence, he alighted on the rooted end of a very old driftwood tree.

"Please allow me to relieve you of your anxieties my dear friends. I can see it in your eyes, Bobby, and you too, Ollie. Yes, this is really me, Reggie."

"Well, that's a relief," said Ollie.

But Bobby, also dumbfounded and struggling to process the situation, simply nodded her huge head.

"For the past few days, I have been searching for any friends who might be able to help me with a particularly bothersome dilemma. You see, I seem to have lost a recent part of my memory. In fact, most of this past winter is missing. I did find Ms. Katie farther down the coast. She was almost invisible as she was crouched and ready to pounce on her next unsuspecting dinner. She forgave me for the intrusion but was unable to help me. Then, for some strange reason, I suddenly felt compelled to return to this beach. I have a very faint and vague memory of having been headed this way some time ago. But that seems to be where my memory lapse begins. I am terribly troubled by my dilemma."

Bobby, having recovered her composure, said, "Well Reggie, you will be very pleased to hear that Ollie and I have detailed information that will help you, at least in part, to reconstruct your missing memory."

So, Bobby and Ollie shared their story of coming upon the crows, their victory dance, and Reggie's disheveled body.

Reggie was totally confounded and confused. He said, "I am having very brief but brilliant flashbacks of something like memories. I vaguely recall gliding around the rocky headland way too low and slow, and flying right into the crows' ambush. I am at a loss to remember how I managed that blunder. And, I am resigned that I must accept your account of the subsequent events verbatim because those memories are obviously lost to me forever. But, I do have a strong and very recent recollection of the small clearing that you described."

"During my most persistent flashback," Reggie explained, "I see myself in a huge screened-in framework of a structure. There is lots of room to hop about. There are many perches at varying heights. The structure is so long that I am able to take off and land. But, there is no way out. My second most frequent bright burst of a vision is of finding herring or salmon always in one corner. The final most frequent glimmer or glint is a very fuzzy and elusive vision of a human. This vision is a bit concerning because this being has somehow gotten into the giant enclosure with me. The image makes no sounds and moves very slowly. Interestingly, the more I think of it now, this apparent delusion or hallucination was always giving off a distinct aura of warmth and compassion; there was no feeling of fear associated with it.

"That is until the final flashback. I was attacked from above and behind. I was suddenly enveloped in a heavy type of blanket or cloth and physically restrained. Even in this horrifying situation, I could feel gentleness and kindness from my captor. In seemingly no time I was suddenly free, no restraints, no confinement, warm, clear, calm air and this small clearing, clear blue skies above. I was free! A vehicle was moving away on an old tractor trail alongside an adjacent abandoned meadow. I have a vivid memory of watching the vehicle drive out of sight. I have total recall of stepping into the clearing and lifting myself into flight. I circled the big old abandoned farm and the surrounding forest. I recognized the familiar coast, the big bay, and the prominent rocky headland. With significant trepidation, I recall the big Douglas fir trees and automatically scanned the upper crowns for those dreaded crows. There were none. I climbed high, circled about, and set off in search of friends, and hopefully answers.

"Then I responded to the irresistible urge to return to this beach."

"And here we are," declared Ollie. "Let's celebrate!"

Bobby just smiled and gave private thanks to the healing spirits. They had worked their wonders yet again.

Epilogue

Dear Reader,

Unlike the other stories, this tall tale, Reggie's Reincarnation, had an unusually long gestation period. Like the interrelated complexities and marvelous mysteries of our natural world, which all these stories emulate, it seemed nearly impossible to figure out how all the essential pieces of this puzzle would ever come together. It was like having this promising jigsaw puzzle missing the motivational picture on the lid of the box.

Then one day, during a chance visit to Wild ARC, the missing inspirational picture magically materialized. This serendipitous encounter proved to be the catalyst that caused the many pieces of this intriguing and compelling puzzle to coalesce into the fanciful fable just shared by our charming characters.

On behalf of our characters and all the wild animals, Reggie's Reincarnation is dedicated to the wonderful workers at British Columbia's Society for the Prevention of Cruelty to Animals (SPCA) and their Wild Animal Rehabilitation Centre (Wild ARC).

Sincerely, Kim